'The pictures in Dr KittyCat
are really funny!'
Poppy, age 7

'I always choose Dr KittyCat for
my bedtime story.'
Isla, age 6

A note from the author:

Jane says...

Our hamster, Tom, often got out
of his cage in my son's bedroom,
but he wasn't interested in
escaping. One night
there was a loud
scream—Tom had
crept into Andy's bed
and snuggled inside
his pyjamas while he
was fast asleep!

Dr KittyCat has taken the little animals on a stargazing trip, and Peanut and Pumpkin have been chosen to carry the telescope. To find out how they get on you had better start the story!

For Tom the hamster—J.C.

OXFORD
UNIVERSITY PRESS

Great Clarendon Street, Oxford OX2 6DP
Oxford University Press is a department of the University of Oxford.
It furthers the University's objective of excellence in research, scholarship,
and education by publishing worldwide

Oxford is a registered trade mark of Oxford University Press
in the UK and in certain other countries

British Library Cataloguing in Publication Data
Data available
ISBN: 978-0-19-274612-2 (paperback)

2 4 6 8 10 9 7 5 3 1

Printed in China by Golden Cup
Paper used in the production of this book is a natural,
recyclable product made from wood grown in sustainable forests.
The manufacturing process conforms to the environmental
regulations of the country of origin.

Dr KittyCat

is ready to rescue

Pumpkin the Hamster

Jane Clarke

OXFORD
UNIVERSITY PRESS

Chapter One

The old-fashioned telephone
on Peanut's desk
began to ring.

Brring! Brring!

Peanut gave a
muffled *eek!*
Supposing someone
needed their help?

He was Dr KittyCat's assistant and
he wasn't ready to rescue! The little
animals were on a first-aid course at
the clinic and Dr KittyCat was using
him to demonstrate bandaging. Peanut
was wrapped in such a long crepe
bandage that he felt like an Egyptian
mummy. Only his ears, whiskers, eyes,
and tail were peeking out.

'Don't panic, Peanut—I'll take the call,' Dr KittyCat told him. She picked up the handset.

All the little animals on the first-aid course fell silent.

'Dr KittyCat's clinic,' she meowed calmly. 'How can we help you?'

Everyone held their breath as Dr KittyCat listened carefully, tilting her furry head and swishing her long tail.

'We'll be happy to,' she purred. She put down the phone.

'Who was it?' Peanut asked. He wasn't having any luck trying to wriggle himself free.

'That was Mrs Hazelnut,'
Dr KittyCat announced. She found
the end of the bandage and began to
unwrap Peanut. 'I'm afraid she can't
take everyone to Heatherhill to stargaze
this evening.'

Posy the puppy, Clover the bunny,
Daisy the kitten, Pumpkin the hamster,
Nutmeg the guinea pig, Sage the owlet,

Bramble the hedgehog, Basil the budgie,
Willow the duckling, and Fennel the
fox cub all looked at one another and
groaned with disappointment.

'She asked Peanut and me to take
over,' Dr KittyCat went on. 'We'll take
all the stargazers to Heatherhill in the
vanbulance.'

The little animals jumped up and down with excitement.

'Yay!' yapped Posy the puppy.

'I love going places in the vanbulance!' Clover the bunny squealed.

'I can't wait to use the telescope,' Pumpkin the hamster squeaked. 'I've never seen the stars properly!'

Dr KittyCat carefully finished unwrapping Peanut from the bandage and turned to the little animals.

'Now find a partner, and take it in turns to practise your bandaging on an elbow, knee, or wrist,' she told them.

There was a bit of a scuffle as everyone formed pairs and decided who would go first.

'Make the casualty comfortable in a sitting or lying position,' Dr KittyCat meowed. 'Bramble, you've rolled yourself into a ball again. That'll make it very hard for Fennel to bandage your leg . . .'

The spiky little hedgehog poked
out his nose and gradually uncurled for
his fox-cub partner.

Dr KittyCat turned to the young
owlet who was carefully placing a
cushion behind the little guinea pig's

back. 'Very good, Sage,' she purred.
'Nutmeg is looking very comfy.'

On the other side of the room,
Daisy gave a little squeal. Peanut
glanced over. Willow the duckling had
a firm grip on the kitten's ear.

'Be gentle. Don't just grab someone and start bandaging,' Peanut reminded everyone. 'Remember, first-aiders reassure the casualty and explain what they are going to do, before they start to do it.'

The clinic echoed with giggles and squeaks as the little animals bandaged one another.

'I finished first!' Pumpkin said proudly. Dr KittyCat and Peanut went over to see. They looked at one another. Pumpkin's partner's leg was a mass of twisted and knotted bandages. It was a terrible mess.

'Posy's paw is looking very pale,'

Dr KittyCat told Pumpkin. 'That means your bandages are too tight. We'd better cut Posy out of them before the blood supply to her foot is cut off and her paw goes numb.'

Peanut handed Dr KittyCat
the tough-cut scissors and watched
her gently snip off the bandage.
He could see the underside of Posy's
paw going back to its normal healthy
pink colour.

Pumpkin's ears drooped.

'You just need a bit more practice
to get it right,' Dr KittyCat said
encouragingly.

Peanut scurried from pair to pair,
checking how everyone was doing.

'Bandage slowly and carefully,'
Dr KittyCat reminded Willow. 'Not
too loose and not too tight. Fennel,
tuck in the ends tidily. Well done,

Basil,' she told the little budgie. 'You've bandaged Clover's elbow beautifully . . .'

'That was a very busy morning,' Peanut squeaked. He rolled up the last of the practice bandages and put them away. Then he picked up the *Furry First-aid Book* and began to note down the names of all the little animals who had attended the course.

Dr KittyCat washed her paws and settled down in her favourite chair. She took her knitting out of her flowery doctor's bag. Peanut glanced at it nervously. Sometimes she knitted things for him—and he didn't always want them. This time, she was making a tiny mitten, and Peanut didn't like mittens very much at all.

'The first-aid course went very well,' Dr KittyCat commented. 'Everyone learned to bandage properly, except for Pumpkin. He needs a lot more practice.'

'He probably wasn't concentrating because he's so excited about going stargazing this evening,' Peanut said.

'I'm excited, too,' Dr KittyCat purred. 'It will be a full moon and a

clear, dark sky. A purr-fect night to look
at the stars.'

'Um, yes, perfect,' Peanut
squeaked. He bent his head over his
book and pretended to be busy writing.
He didn't like to tell Dr KittyCat that
he wasn't very happy or excited about
going stargazing. He hadn't told anyone
that he was afraid of the dark!

Chapter Two

It was a cold, dark evening. Peanut's whiskers were already beginning to quiver and they hadn't even got started yet. A group of excited little animals wearing woolly gloves, scarves, and hats gathered beside the vanbulance.

'Do we have the stargazing telescope and stand?' Dr KittyCat asked him.

'They're in the back,' Peanut squeaked. 'Mrs Hazelnut brought them round and helped me load them into the vanbulance.' He shivered. 'How many torches do we have?' he asked.

'I have a headlamp,' Fennel piped up.

'So do I,' peeped Basil.

'And me!' said Pumpkin

'And I brought a lantern!' Willow quacked proudly.

They switched on their torches and beams of light lit up the flowers that Peanut had painted on the vanbulance. Peanut clicked on his pencil torch. The light wobbled as the torch shook in his paw.

Dr KittyCat looked concerned. 'You're cold, Peanut,' she meowed. 'You need a pair of mittens to keep your paws warm tonight.' She delved into her flowery doctor's bag. 'Here, have the ones I just finished knitting. They're mouse-sized. And I have a stripy scarf in here, too.'

Peanut wrapped the woolly scarf around his neck and pulled on the mittens. He immediately felt warmer—and braver. Maybe mittens weren't so bad after all!

'Thanks!' he squeaked.

'Are we ready to go?' asked Dr KittyCat. 'It feels as if we've forgotten something . . .'

'Your bag!' Peanut exclaimed. 'We didn't check to make sure everything was in it!'

'We can do that now.' Dr KittyCat quickly reopened her flowery doctor's bag. Peanut shone his torch into it so that she could inspect the contents.

'Scissors, syringe, medicines, ointments, instant cool packs, paw-cleansing gel, wipes,' she murmured.
'Stethoscope, ophthalmoscope, thermometer, tweezers, bandages, gauze, sticking plasters, peppermint lozenges, tongue depressor, headlamp... and reward stickers. It's all here,' she announced. 'We're ready to rescue if there's an emergency!'

Dr KittyCat opened the side door of the vanbulance.

'It's time to go. Hop in, everyone,' she meowed.

Posy, Clover, Daisy, Pumpkin, Nutmeg, Sage, Bramble, Basil, Willow, and Fennel piled onto the bench seats at the back of the vanbulance. Peanut checked their seatbelts were secure, closed the door and scampered round to the passenger seat. He carefully pulled his tail out of the way before he closed his door and pulled on his belt. Beside him, in the driver's seat, Dr KittyCat did the same.

'Ready to roll?' she asked.

'Ready to roll!' chorused the little animals in the back.

Peanut pressed the siren button on the dashboard.

Nee-nah! Nee—

'Oops,' Peanut squeaked, quickly switching it off. 'It's not an emergency!'

Dr KittyCat turned the key. There was a *vroom, vroom, vroom,* and the vanbulance slowly pulled away from the clinic.

'There are so many in the back, I'll have to drive a lot more slowly than usual, or they'll bounce all over the place,' Dr KittyCat explained.

Peanut sighed with relief. Dr KittyCat's fast driving often made him panic. He gazed out of the window. A bright moon was coming up, and he didn't feel scared at all as the vanbulance rattled across the timber bridge. They rounded Duckpond Bend on all four wheels for a change, and rumbled through Thistletown. He only began to feel nervous when they left the town behind. The windy country road up

Heatherhill was lined with tall trees that were swaying in the wind. Spooky moon shadows squirmed across the road. Peanut's heart began to beat faster. He stifled an *eek!* and closed his eyes. He breathed slowly in and out as Dr KittyCat had taught him to do when he felt panicky, and tried to imagine himself in his favourite place full of his favourite things . . .

a cheese shop packed full of different
cheeses.

He was just imagining sinking
his teeth into a lovely nutty piece of
cheddar when Dr KittyCat brought the
vanbulance to a halt.

'This is as far as we can go in the
vanbulance,' she announced. 'We'll walk
the rest of the way to the top of the
hill. Luckily, it's a clear night with no
cloud cover. There will be a purr-fect
view of the night sky.'

Peanut opened his eyes and peered
around him. The dark blue sky was
sprinkled with tiny stars and curved
away as if it went on for ever. He wasn't

34

at all sure he wanted to get out of the
vanbulance. The night sky was so big for
such a little mouse. Especially a mouse
who was scared of the dark!

Chapter Three

Peanut tried to think of cheese as
Dr KittyCat opened the doors and the
little animals scrambled out of the
vanbulance. No one else seemed to think
it was dark and scary outside.

'Can you and Pumpkin
manage to carry the
telescope?'

Dr KittyCat asked Peanut. 'Fennel and Posy can bring the stand.'

Peanut nodded. He didn't like to speak in case his teeth started chattering with fear.

'Mrs Hazelnut told me the best place to set up,' Dr KittyCat told them all. 'Follow me.' She picked up her flowery doctor's bag and led the way towards a clump of trees.

Peanut and Pumpkin pulled the telescope out of the vanbulance and set off with Peanut at the front and Pumpkin at the back. The ground was humpy and bumpy and springy with heather. It was hard for Peanut to see

where he was going because his paws
were too full of telescope for him to
switch on his torch. He stared nervously
into the gloom, and heard an eerie
rustling noise from the trees ahead
of them.

Peanut's heart jumped into his mouth and he froze to the spot. 'Eek!' he squealed. 'What's that?'

'Don't panic, Peanut, it's only the wind whistling through the leaves,' Dr KittyCat meowed calmly. 'We don't have far to go now—the best stargazing spot is just on the other side of the trees.'

Peanut's knees were trembling. He took a deep breath and carried on. Suddenly, there was a *thump!* and the end of the telescope dropped to the ground. Peanut whirled round. Why had Pumpkin dropped it? He could see the light from Pumpkin's headlamp pooling on the ground.

'Are you OK?' Peanut rushed over
to him. The little hamster was face
down in a clump of springy heather.

'I'm fine. I just stumbled over something,' Pumpkin said, getting slowly to his feet.

Dr KittyCat quickly checked him over. 'No damage done, unless you count a bit of dirt,' she smiled.

'I'll take the end of the telescope while you catch your breath, Pumpkin,' Basil volunteered.

'Thanks!' Pumpkin brushed himself down and readjusted his headlamp. 'I'll follow on behind.'

'Watch where you are going, everyone,' Dr KittyCat called. 'There are a lot of fallen branches around here. Mrs Hazelnut said that some trees were blown down by last year's storm.'

There was enough light for Peanut to make out the shapes of branches lying on the ground.

He was stepping carefully over a large twig when there was a loud *Squ-eee-ak!*

Everyone froze.

42

'Who was that?' Dr KittyCat meowed.

A tiny voice came out of the darkness.

'It's me—Pumpkin! I've hurt myself!' he whimpered.

Peanut and Basil put down the telescope. The little animals shone their torches into the night.

'Where is he?' Peanut panicked. 'I can't see him. His headlamp's gone out!'

There was another *squ-eee-ak!* from the direction of the trees.

'I fell down a hole,' Pumpkin wailed.

It still wasn't clear where
Pumpkin's voice was coming from.
Peanut and the other little animals
shone their torches across the bumpy,
branch-strewn ground. Peanut spotted
Pumpkin's headlamp. He picked it up
and switched it back on. It still worked.

'I'm down here!' Pumpkin squeaked again.

'We'll be there in a whisker!' Dr KittyCat called, following the sound and being careful not to fall over. Once she had found the spot, Peanut and the other little animals slowly followed and gathered round. Pumpkin was lying on his back at the bottom of a hole left by an uprooted young tree. The hole was small, but quite deep, and Pumpkin was covered in leaves.

'We're here now, Pumpkin,' Dr KittyCat called. 'Everything will be fine.' She turned to Peanut. 'I'm too big to get in this little hole,' she told him.

'You'll have to go down and examine him before we try to get him out.'

Peanut nodded. He knew how important it was not to move a patient before all the right checks had been made. But the hole was very, very dark. The thought of it made his whiskers quiver and his knees knock. Peanut's heart began to beat faster. Dare he climb down into the dark?

Chapter Four

Peanut took a deep breath. 'I'm a furry first-aider,' he told himself. 'I can't let Pumpkin and Dr KittyCat down.'

His paws shook as he took off his mittens and pulled on Pumpkin's headlamp.

'Shine your torches here,' he squeaked.

The little animals focused beams
of light on the hole. Peanut could see
tiny tree roots poking out the sides,
like a mass of wriggly worms. Peanut
gulped. His heart thumped wildly
as he scrambled down the
peaty sides of the hole. But
the instant he was beside
Pumpkin, he forgot to be
scared of the dark.
He was ready to
rescue.

'You're safe in our paws,' he reassured Pumpkin as he brushed the leaf mould away from the little hamster. Peanut gave a sigh of relief. Pumpkin didn't look as if he was badly injured.

'Can you tell me where it hurts?' Peanut asked.

'It's my ankle,' Pumpkin moaned.

'Don't forget to check to make sure Pumpkin hasn't hurt his head, back, or neck,' Dr KittyCat called down.

'My head is fine,' Pumpkin groaned, as Peanut examined him and checked he was breathing normally.

'I need to check you all over

before I can move you,' Peanut squeaked. He knew just what to do. 'Can you wiggle your fingers and toes for me?' he asked. He watched as Pumpkin wiggled all four paws.

'Very good,' he told Pumpkin. 'Now, try to move your tail a tiny bit.'

The hamster's stubby little tail twitched. Peanut smiled.

'I think Pumpkin's only hurt his ankle,' Peanut called up to Dr KittyCat.

'Good. You're doing really well, both of you,' Dr KittyCat meowed down. 'Now Peanut, I need you to gently run your paws over Pumpkin's ankle and tell me if it feels twisted or swollen or hot, or out of place at all.'

'Don't worry. I'll be very gentle,'
Peanut told Pumpkin as he followed
Dr KittyCat's instructions.

'My ankle doesn't hurt much
now,' Pumpkin told him. 'It's just a bit
sore and achy.'

'Pumpkin's ankle feels fine to me,' Peanut called up to Dr KittyCat. 'He says it doesn't hurt so much now.'

'It doesn't sound as if Pumpkin has broken his ankle,' Dr KittyCat meowed. 'I think he probably has a mild sprain from turning his ankle awkwardly when he fell down the hole.'

'Can I get out of here now?' asked Pumpkin.

'Peanut just needs to do one more test to make certain it's safe to move you,' Dr KittyCat called. 'He'll use the ophthalmoscope. I'm lowering it down now.'

Peanut reached up and took the ophthalmoscope from Dr KittyCat's outstretched paw. The special doctor's instrument was for examining eyes without dazzling the patient.

'I'm going to look in both of your eyes to make sure you won't get dizzy when you move,' Peanut told Pumpkin. He carefully held the ophthalmoscope to each eye in turn.

'Pumpkin's eyes look fine,' Peanut squeaked. 'You can pull him out now!'

Peanut flattened himself against the side of the hole as Dr KittyCat stretched down her furry paw.

Pumpkin grabbed hold of it and Dr KittyCat hoisted him up.

Peanut scrambled out of the hole. Pumpkin was sitting on the ground next to it, while Dr KittyCat gently examined his ankle. Peanut gave the headlamp back to Pumpkin, then carefully replaced the ophthalmoscope in Dr KittyCat's bag, brushed the earth off his scarf and fur, and put his mittens back on.

'Thank you, Peanut,' Dr KittyCat murmured. 'You did very well down there. I don't know what I'd do without you.'

Peanut felt his ears go pink.

'How are you doing?' he asked the little hamster.

Pumpkin burst into tears. 'I didn't see where I was going!' he wailed. 'And now I'm spoiling the stargazing for everyone.'

'There, there,' Dr KittyCat purred.

'Everyone can carry on looking at the stars. It's only a mild sprain. You'll soon be as good as new again. We'll bandage you up like you learned to do in the first-aid class this morning.'

'Can I do it?' Basil peeped.

'You said my bandaging is very tidy.'

'My bandaging is very good, too,' Posy yapped.

'And mine,' hooted Sage. 'I'd like to bandage Pumpkin's ankle. Let me do it, pl-eee-ase!'

'It's wonderful to have so many volunteers,' Dr KittyCat said, smiling, 'but I think Peanut should put on the support bandage. He's shown us all what he can do tonight, and he's an expert at bandaging, too.'

Peanut felt as if he would burst with pride.

'While you do that, I'll set up the telescope,' Dr KittyCat told him.

The little animals gathered round as Peanut opened Dr KittyCat's bag and took out a bandage. He unrolled the end and held it in place on Pumpkin's foot. Then he carefully unravelled the bandage as he wrapped it over and

over in a neat figure of eight around
Pumpkin's ankle and foot. He made
sure it was not too tight and not too
loose and tucked in the end tidily.

'You shouldn't put too much
weight on your ankle for a day or two,'
Peanut told Pumpkin. 'Sit here for a
moment with your leg raised while
I find you a pair of walking sticks.'

Peanut scampered over to the
fallen branches and found two
hamster-height twigs with a
V-shaped end.

'Put the V shapes under your arms
and lean on these,' he told Pumpkin.

Everyone clapped paws and wings

as he helped Pumpkin to his feet.

'There's just one more thing
I have to do,' Peanut remembered.
He rummaged in Dr KittyCat's
flowery doctor's bag and found
Pumpkin a sticker that said: 'I was
a purr-fect patient for Dr KittyCat!'

I was a purr-fect patient for Dr KittyCat!

Pumpkin smiled as Peanut stuck it on his bobble hat.

'Now it's time to do some stargazing,' Peanut announced, and he led the youngsters to the stargazing spot where Dr KittyCat was waiting.

'Good work, Peanut!' Dr KittyCat purred as she examined Peanut's work. 'That's the purr-fect bandage.'

She turned to the little hamster. 'Pumpkin, I think you should have the first turn at the telescope.'

Pumpkin hobbled up.

'The planet Venus is the brightest star in the sky tonight,' Dr KittyCat told everyone. 'It's very easy to spot.'

'I can't see it,' Pumpkin squeaked. 'The sky looks all fuzzy.'

'There must be paw prints on the lens of the telescope,' Peanut murmured. He took a piece of gauze from Dr KittyCat's bag and polished the circular glass. He put his eye to the telescope and gazed at the night sky. Venus looked huge! It was wonderfully sparkly.

'I can see Venus clearly,' he said. 'Take another look, Pumpkin.'

Pumpkin pressed his eye to the lens and screwed up his furry face in concentration.

'It's still all blurry,' he said.

Peanut's tummy gave a lurch. He shone his torch on the *Furry First-aid*

Book and flipped through it. 'Eek!' he squeaked. 'Things can look blurry when you've been hit on the head! Pumpkin said his head was fine, so I didn't check to see if there were any bumps or bruises. I must have missed something!'

Chapter Five

'Don't panic, Peanut,' Dr KittyCat
meowed calmly. 'We can work
this out. Do you have a headache,
Pumpkin?'

Pumpkin shook his head.

Dr KittyCat looked him over
carefully. 'There are no signs of any
bumps or scrapes or bruises on your

head, and your eyes look fine,' she
murmured.

'I have a bruise on my knee,'
Pumpkin said helpfully. 'That's from
when I tripped over the first time.'

'Why did you trip over, do you
think?' Dr KittyCat asked him.

'I couldn't see where I was going.'

'That's not surprising. It's very dark,' Peanut squeaked.

'But *you* could see enough to step over those branches, couldn't you, Peanut?' Dr KittyCat said thoughtfully. 'And so could I—and so could Bramble and the others.'

Everyone nodded in agreement.

Dr KittyCat looked serious for a moment. Then her eyes sparkled like the stars in the sky.

'Your head is fine, Pumpkin,' she meowed.

'So what is wrong with him?' Peanut squeaked.

'There's nothing wrong,'
Dr KittyCat purred happily. 'Pumpkin just doesn't see as clearly as some of us do, that's all.'

'It's his eyesight!' Peanut gave a big sigh of relief. 'I thought he was tripping over things because it was dark, but it was because he couldn't see very well. That's probably why his bandaging was so untidy, too.'

'It's easy to fix, Pumpkin,'
Dr KittyCat reassured the worried-looking hamster. 'All you need is a pair of glasses.'

'But I don't want to wear glasses,' Pumpkin howled. 'Everyone will laugh at me.'

'No one in Thistletown would be that unkind.' Dr KittyCat looked at the small animals. 'You won't laugh, will you?'

They shook their heads solemnly. Pumpkin gave a watery smile.

'Good,' said Dr KittyCat. 'Now, who wants a turn to look through the telescope?'

There was a chorus of *'Me, me, me!'* as all the little animals except Pumpkin dashed to form a line.

'From up here, you can see lots of stars even without a telescope,' Dr KittyCat told the stargazers as they waited for their turn.

They all gazed up at the glittering sky.
'We're looking at the Milky Way,'
Dr KittyCat explained. 'That's a galaxy
of stars.'

Pumpkin sighed as everyone *oohed*
and *aahed*.

'I'm sorry you're missing out on the

stargazing,' Peanut told Pumpkin. 'Let's practise walking with sticks and keeping your poorly foot off the ground.' He picked up two mouse-sized sticks and the two of them hopped around the springy heather.

'This is fun!' Pumpkin squeaked.

'It is,' agreed Peanut and he suddenly realized that he'd been so busy, he'd totally forgotten he was afraid of the dark. He wasn't scared at all!

'What an exciting night it's been,' Dr KittyCat purred as they packed everything and everyone back into the vanbulance.

'It was amazing!' Peanut agreed. He was worn out by all the excitement, and so was everyone else. One by one, the tired little animals fell asleep as Dr KittyCat drove carefully back to Thistletown. Peanut's head nodded

against his chin. He wished he was in
his comfortable bed in the special cabin
in the roof of the vanbulance. He never
felt relaxed enough to sleep in the front
seat when Dr KittyCat was driving . . .

zzz . . . zzz . . . zzz . . .

'Wake up everyone, we're back at the clinic,' Dr KittyCat called.

Peanut shook himself awake. He'd been dreaming of being a taste-tester in a cheese factory. It was almost as good a job as being a first-aider.

'I went to sleep while you were driving,' he gasped in disbelief.

'You certainly did,' Dr KittyCat laughed. 'You were snoring the loudest of all!'

The sleepy little animals said goodnight and set off for their homes.

'Pumpkin, come to the clinic tomorrow for an eye test,' Dr KittyCat told him. 'Once I have the results, I shall be able to order a special pair of glasses for you. When you wear them, your eyesight will be even better than mine!'

Chapter Six

It was one week later. Peanut peeked out of the clinic window.

'There's a very long line of youngsters outside,' he squeaked. 'It's not a special day at the clinic and none of them look poorly. I wonder why they've come to see us?'

'There's only one way to find out,'

Dr KittyCat meowed. She pulled on
her white coat and opened the door.

'How can we help?' she asked.

Sage was at the front of the line.

'We've all come to have our eyes tested,
like Pumpkin,' Sage announced.

'That's a good idea,' Dr KittyCat purred. 'Everyone should have their eyesight checked regularly. Eyes are so important. It will only take a moment for us to get everything ready.'

Peanut rushed around helping Dr KittyCat set out her eyesight chart, the eyedrops, the ophthalmoscope, and the special glasses she used to test how well each eye was working.

'Ready!' he announced.

Sage hopped into the chair.

'First of all, I shall put drops in your eyes,' Dr KittyCat told her. 'It won't hurt at all. It makes the pupils bigger so I can see into your eyes better.

Tip your head back a little.'

Peanut handed Dr KittyCat the eyedrops and she gently squeezed a drop into each of Sage's eyes. The little owlet blinked.

'Next, I shall look at the back
of each eye to check that they are
focusing properly. Stay nice and still.'
Dr KittyCat peered through the
ophthalmoscope.

'That's very good, Sage. Now it's
time for the eyesight charts, Peanut.'

'I have them right here.' Peanut
took the rolled-up charts and
scampered to the end of the room.
He chose one and held it up. The chart
was covered with pictures of different
animals. They were in lines, the biggest
at the top and tiny ones at the bottom.

'Tell us what animals you can see,
Sage,' he squeaked.

'I can see them all,' Sage hooted.

Peanut pointed to outlines of tiny animals on the bottom line of the chart.

Sage rattled them off. 'Rabbit, snail, butterfly, mouse.'

'Purr-fect,' Dr KittyCat purred. 'The final part of the test is to make sure you can see equally well out of both eyes. To do that, I need to cover up each eye in turn.'

She took a pair of glasses with one lens open and one lens like a pirate's patch and popped them on Sage's beak.

Peanut held up a different chart for Sage to read. She gave the names of all the animals on it. Dr KittyCat moved the patch to the other side of the glasses and Sage repeated the test with her other eye.

'Your eyesight is fine, Sage,' Dr KittyCat confirmed with a smile. 'You don't need to wear glasses.'

'I don't?' Sage sounded a bit disappointed. 'But I can have a sticker, can't I?'

'Of course.' Dr KittyCat took one from her bag.

Sage hopped happily down from the chair and shuffled her feathers.

'Next!' she announced. Posy bounded eagerly in.

Dr KittyCat and Peanut were rushed off their feet testing all the little animals. All of them had perfect eyesight—and all of them wanted stickers. They were about to put everything away when Pumpkin turned up.

'I love your glasses!' Dr KittyCat meowed. 'They look really cute on you!'

'I've only been wearing them a day, but everyone I've met says that,' Pumpkin grinned. 'No one's laughed. I think they're all a bit jealous.'

'That would explain why everyone turned up today wanting an eye test,' Dr KittyCat giggled. 'They all want glasses, too.'

'Glasses are brilliant!' Pumpkin exclaimed. 'I can see everything clearly now. Before, I thought everyone saw the world like I did, with fuzzy edges. No wonder I fell over all the time.'

'How's your ankle?' asked Peanut. 'It's good to see you don't have sticks or a bandage any more. But I hope that's not because my bandage fell off.'

'It didn't! I took it off because my ankle's completely better now,' Pumpkin told him. 'I came in to say thank you—and to show you my new glasses, of course.'

'It's lovely to see you looking so well,' Dr KittyCat purred. 'And it's all thanks to Peanut!'

'It wasn't just me,' Peanut said modestly as Pumpkin waved goodbye.

'You were very brave that night,' Dr KittyCat went on. 'Especially since you were so afraid of the dark.'

'I didn't think you knew!' squeaked Peanut.

'I did,' smiled Dr KittyCat, 'but it didn't make me think less of you. In fact, it made me even prouder to be your friend.'

Peanut gave a happy sigh as he
took out the *Furry First-aid Book* to
finish the section on Pumpkin's ankle
and write up the results of the eye tests.
A picture of a very happy Pumpkin
wearing his new glasses popped into his
mind.

*Pumpkin's glasses would look cool
and cute on me,* Peanut thought.

He scrunched up his eyes and peered at the words he was writing. Was it his imagination or did they look a bit blurry?

'Do you think I need glasses?' he asked Dr KittyCat hopefully.

'There's only one way to find out,' laughed Dr KittyCat as she unrolled the eyesight chart.

The end

What to take on your very own stargazing trip!

Even if you don't have a telescope, you can have a lot of fun going out and looking up at the stars. Here are some of the things that Dr KittyCat would take.

Warm clothes

It gets cold when the sun goes down and the stars come out, so make sure you're wearing something warm!

Food and drink

It can be thirsty work looking at the stars – why not take a thermos flask of soup or a hot drink to keep you warm?

Torch

It's harder to see when it's dark, as Peanut and Pumpkin find out! Take a torch with you to help you see, and so that you don't fall over!

Blanket

If you lie down on a blanket and look up you can see even more of the sky, and you won't get a sore neck. Just be careful you don't fall asleep!

If you loved Pumpkin the Hamster, here's an extract from another Dr KittyCat adventure:

Dr KittyCat is ready to rescue: Nutmeg the Guinea Pig

This time Dr KittyCat is helping a little guinea pig called Nutmeg who is feeling poorly at her birthday party in the park . . .

Dr KittyCat knelt down beside Nutmeg. 'You're safe in our paws,' she reassured her. 'Peanut and I will soon find out what's wrong and make you feel better. Can you tell us how you are feeling now?'

Nutmeg slowly opened her eyes and looked up.

'Ugh!' she gasped. 'My lips feel all

clammy. I think I'm going to be sick . . .'
She closed her eyes again.

Peanut glanced towards the ice
cream van. 'Have you been eating a lot
of ice cream?' he asked.

'I have!' Posy yapped. 'I've had
three vanilla cones already!'

'That would make me feel really
sick,' Peanut squeaked. 'What about
you, Nutmeg?'

Ugh

Here are some other stories that we think you'll love!